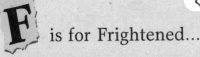 is for Frightened...

Suddenly, Josh stopped. "Listen!" he said.

Josh knelt next to a patch of tangled weeds. Slowly, he parted the stalks with his fingers.

A brown bird was hunched in the weeds. It had a sharp beak and shiny black eyes.

"It's a peregrine falcon!" Josh said.

"The poor thing looks scared," Ruth Rose said.

Josh took off his T-shirt and carefully draped it over the bird. "He won't be so scared if he can't see us," Josh explained. He held the bundle against his chest.

"Hey, what's this?" Josh said. He gently stretched out one of the falcon's legs.

Wrapped around the leg was a narrow metal band...

The **A** to **Z Mysteries**™ series!

The Absent Author
The Bald Bandit
The Canary Caper
The Deadly Dungeon
The Empty Envelope
The Falcon's Feathers

*This book is dedicated to all kids who like
animals and respect nature
–R.R.*

*To Ian Campbell
–J.S.G.*

ISBN 0-590-05203-3

Text copyright © 1998 by Ron Roy.
Illustrations copyright © 1998 by John Steven Gurney.
All rights reserved. Published by Scholastic Inc.,
557 Broadway, New York, NY 10012, by arrangement with
Random House Children's Books, a division of Random House, Inc.

60 59 58 57 56 55 54 53 52 51 50   18 19 20/0

Printed in the U.S.A.   40

First Scholastic printing, March 1999

A to Z Mysteries™

The Falcon's Feathers

by Ron Roy

illustrated by
John Steven Gurney

SCHOLASTIC INC.

New York   Toronto   London   Auckland   Sydney
Mexico City   New Delhi   Hong Kong   Buenos Aires

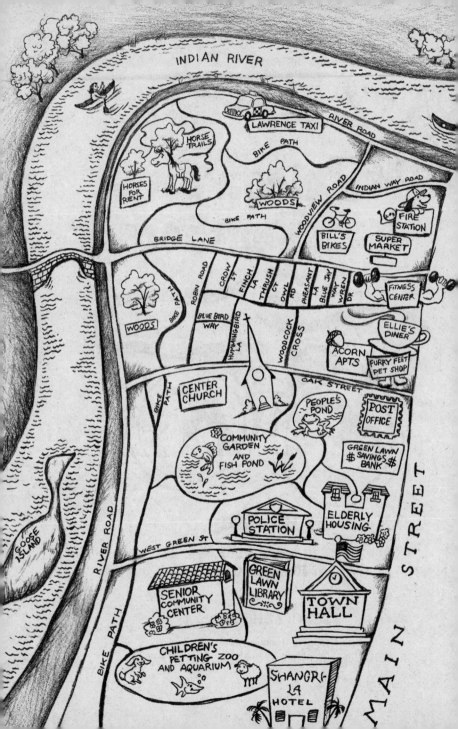

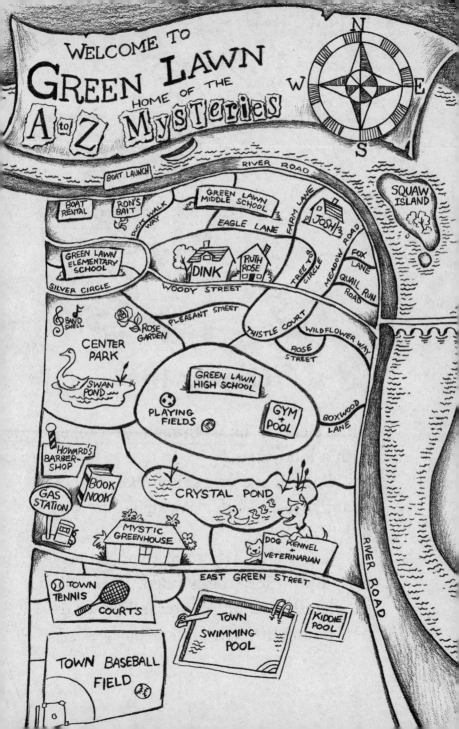

Chapter 1

Dink stepped on a branch. It broke with a loud snap.

"Geez, Dink, you sound like an elephant!" Josh said. "We have to be quiet!"

"Josh Pinto, where are you taking us?" Ruth Rose demanded. "I'm all scratches! Why didn't you tell us we'd be walking through pricker bushes?"

The kids were deep in the woods, not far from the horse trails. The bushes were thick under the tall trees.

Josh grinned at his friends. "It's a surprise," he said. "Trust me, you'll love it."

"Well, I don't love all these mosquitoes," Dink muttered.

Ruth Rose sat on a log and scratched a bite on her ankle. "I'm not going any farther until you spill the beans," she said.

"Me neither," Dink said. He plopped down next to Ruth Rose. "Out with it, Josh. Why'd you drag us into this jungle?"

"And what's with the binoculars?" Ruth Rose asked.

"Okay, I'll tell you." Josh squeezed between them on the log and pulled a piece of paper from his pocket. He spread it out across his knees.

It was a drawing of a bird. It had dark feathers, a curved beak, and black markings under the eyes.

"What is it?" asked Dink. "An eagle?"

Josh shook his head. "No, it's a peregrine falcon. They were almost extinct—but now there's a family in Green Lawn!"

Dink was impressed. "Did *you* draw this?"

Josh nodded. "Yup. I found a nest with three babies. I've been watching them for a couple of weeks now."

"And you're just telling us today?" Ruth Rose said. "Thanks for sharing, Josh."

Josh folded the drawing and stuck it in his pocket. "Falcons don't like to be disturbed," he said. "I was waiting to tell you when the babies were older."

Dink looked over their heads at the trees. "So where's the nest?" he asked.

Josh stood up. "We're almost there," he said.

The kids picked their way through the undergrowth. Between the branches, Dink could see glimpses of the Indian River.

A minute later, Josh stopped. "It's right over there," he whispered. "The tall tree in the clearing."

"All I see are leaves," Ruth Rose said.

Josh pointed about halfway up the tree. "See that brown stuff right over the dead branch?"

"I see it!" Ruth Rose cried.

"Me too," Dink said. "How did you climb up there?"

"I didn't," said Josh. "If you disturb the nest, the parents might abandon the babies."

Josh pointed to a white birch tree at the edge of the clearing. "I climb that tree and look over with my binoculars."

"Can we climb up and take a look?" Ruth Rose asked.

"Sure," Josh said. "Only we have to be quiet. I don't want to scare them."

The birch tree was perfect for climbing. The smooth limbs made a natural ladder. Dink and Ruth Rose followed Josh up to a thick branch.

Josh trained his binoculars on the other tree. He adjusted the focus by turning a little wheel between the two eyepieces.

"That's weird," he muttered.

"What's weird?" Ruth Rose asked.

"Let me see." Dink took the glasses and squinted through the lenses. From his perch, Dink could see directly into the nest. It was woven of twigs, pine needles, and bits of dead leaves.

But there weren't any falcons. All Dink could see was a few feathers.

He looked at Josh with raised eyebrows.

"Where are they?" he asked.

"What's going on?" Ruth Rose asked.

Josh looked at her. "The baby falcons are gone."

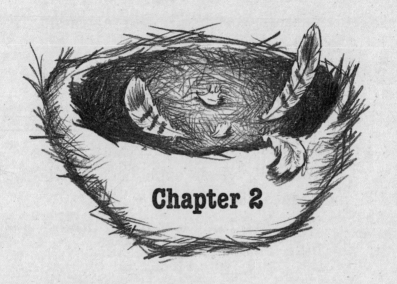

Chapter 2

"Maybe they flew away," Ruth Rose suggested.

The kids had climbed down and were standing under the falcons' tree.

Josh shook his head. "They were just learning to fly," he said. "They weren't ready to leave their parents yet."

"Could they have fallen out?" Dink asked. He glanced at the ground.

"I doubt it," said Josh. "If they had, the parents would still be here, watching over them."

He frowned. "I think something took those birds," he said.

"What do you mean?" Ruth Rose asked. "What kind of something?"

"Animals," Josh explained. "Owls and snakes like to eat baby birds."

"But wouldn't the parents protect the little falcons?" Dink asked.

"Yeah," Josh said. "Unless something happened to them, too."

"Maybe something scared the parents away," Ruth Rose said.

Josh shook his head. "The parents wouldn't leave their babies."

"Then what could have happened to them?" Dink asked. "Five falcons can't just disappear!"

"I don't know," Josh said. He looked worried. "Come on, let's get out

of here. I want to report this."

"Report it to who?" Ruth Rose asked. She and Dink followed Josh back toward the path.

"I'm not sure. But we can ask Mrs. Wong," said Josh. "She knows a lot about animals."

Twenty minutes later, the kids walked into Furry Feet, Mrs. Wong's pet shop. She was cleaning a large goldfish tank.

"Hi, kids," Mrs. Wong said. "What's up? I was just about to close for the day."

Josh explained about the missing falcons. "They were there yesterday," he said, "but today they're gone!"

Mrs. Wong wiped her hands on her jeans. "That does seem odd," she said.

"Peregrines are an endangered species," Josh said. "Should I report this to someone?"

"That's a good idea, Josh," said Mrs. Wong. She went over to her desk and pulled open a drawer.

"Here you go," she said, handing

Josh a card. "That's the number for the Department of Environmental Protection—the DEP, for short. They have an office over at the fire station."

"Thanks, Mrs. Wong," Josh said. "May I use your phone?"

Josh dialed the number while Mrs. Wong went back to cleaning the goldfish tank.

Dink and Ruth Rose listened as Josh explained about the nest and the missing falcons. He thanked whomever he was speaking with and hung up.

"Someone is gonna go out there and take a look," he told Dink and Ruth Rose. "But the guy I talked to said an owl probably got the babies."

Ruth Rose shuddered. "Those poor falcons!"

The kids thanked Mrs. Wong and left the store.

Outside, it was starting to get dark. Ruth Rose, Josh, and Dink crossed Main Street and cut through Center Park. A family of ducks was swimming in the pond. When the parents noticed the humans, they quacked loudly to

their babies. The ducklings quickly swam over to their mother and father.

Josh stopped walking. "I don't think an owl could have taken those baby falcons."

"You don't?" Dink asked.

Josh shook his head. "Mother and father falcons are fierce! They wouldn't let an owl within ten feet of their nest."

"Could a snake climb that high?" Ruth Rose asked.

Josh smirked. "Yeah, a human snake!"

"What do you mean?" Dink asked. "You think a *person* stole the falcons?"

Josh nodded.

"But who would do something like that?" Ruth Rose asked.

"I don't know," Josh said. "But we're going to find out!"

Chapter 3

The next morning, Dink rang Ruth Rose's doorbell. She came to the door wearing a green jogging suit. Even her sneakers and headband were green.

"You look like a bush," Dink said.

Ruth Rose grinned and yelled into the house, "MOM, I'M LEAVING!"

She and Dink headed up Woody Street to pick up Josh. They were going back to the falcons' nest to look for clues.

Josh lived at the end of Farm Lane, in a big yellow house. Behind the house stood a white barn. Josh was shooting baskets at a hoop nailed to the barn door.

He was dressed in a camouflage shirt and pants.

"Geez," Dink said, "why didn't you guys tell me you were going disguised as trees!"

The three kids hurried down River Road, then took a bike path into the woods. Just before they reached the clearing, Josh stopped. A man wearing jeans and a flannel shirt was standing under the falcons' tree, looking up into the branches.

The kids looked at each other, then stepped into the clearing.

The man turned around. He had wavy black hair, a tanned face, and blue eyes.

"Hi there," the man said. "What are you kids up to?"

"We were just hiking," Josh said cautiously.

The man smiled. "Wait a minute. Your voice is awfully familiar. Are you the guy who called my office yesterday about the missing falcons?"

Josh grinned. "Yeah, that was me,"

he said. Josh introduced himself. "And these are my friends, Dink and Ruth Rose."

"Very nice to meet you," the man said. "My name's Curt. Look, guys, I know you want to help, but the best thing you can do is to stay away from here. The adult falcons won't come back if they see or smell you kids."

"But we came back to look for clues," Josh said. "I thought a person might have taken the falcons."

Curt looked surprised. "A person? Well, it's possible, I suppose. But I doubt it. I've been over this whole area, and I didn't find a single clue, human or otherwise."

The kids followed Curt as he walked away from the tree. "The DEP appreciates your phone call," Curt said, "but leave the rest to us. I have a feeling we'll wrap this up soon."

At the trail, Curt turned right. "Thanks again!" he said. He waved and began jogging down the path.

The kids headed down the trail in the other direction. Suddenly, Josh stopped. "Listen!" he said.

"What?" Ruth Rose said.

"I heard something." Josh knelt next to a patch of tangled weeds. Slowly, he parted the stalks with his fingers.

A brown bird was hunched in the weeds. It had a sharp beak and shiny black eyes.

"It's a young peregrine falcon!" Josh said. "He must be from the nest!"

The bird was trembling. It opened its beak and made *cack-cack-cack* noises at Josh. Its shiny eyes never left Josh's face.

"The poor thing looks scared," Ruth Rose said.

Josh took off his T-shirt and carefully draped it over the bird. "He won't be so scared if he can't see us," Josh explained. He held the bundle against his chest.

"What should we do with it?" Dink asked.

"We can't leave him here," Josh said. "Something will eat him."

"Let's take him to Mrs. Wong!" Ruth Rose said.

The kids hurried down the path. Josh smoothed the bird's feathers and spoke to it in a soothing voice.

"Hey, what's this?" Josh said. He gently stretched out one of the falcon's legs.

Wrapped around the leg was a narrow metal band.

Chapter 4

Mrs. Wong examined the band. "There's writing on it," she told the kids. "But it's too small for me to read."

"What is it?" Josh asked.

"It's a name tag," said Mrs. Wong. "Just like you'd hang on a dog's collar. Someone thinks he owns this bird."

Josh was holding the falcon, still partly wrapped in his T-shirt. It sat quietly, watching the humans.

"I wonder if he's hungry," Ruth Rose said. "What do falcons eat?"

"Peregrines mostly eat other birds," Josh said. "But they'll eat fish and other stuff, too."

"Let's find out!" said Mrs. Wong. She opened a small refrigerator and pulled out some raw hamburger. She pinched off a chunk and held it under the falcon's beak.

"Come on, take it," Josh murmured.

Suddenly, the falcon's head shot forward. In one quick gulp, the meat was gone.

"Boy, I guess he was hungry!" Ruth Rose said. "We should name him Flash!"

Flash began making a loud, piercing call. He shrieked over and over until Mrs. Wong fed him another piece of hamburger meat. After the second helping, he stopped fussing and closed his eyes.

"What should we do with him?" Josh asked Mrs. Wong.

She reached for the phone. "For starters, we should ask Doc Henry to look him over."

The kids listened as Mrs. Wong told the veterinarian about Flash. She hung up the phone and said, "He'll take a look if you kids bring the bird to his office. He's right over on East Green Street."

Josh bundled Flash into his shirt again, and the kids hurried to Doc Henry's office.

While Josh washed his hands, Doc Henry examined Flash. "And you found this guy where?" Doc Henry asked.

"Out in the woods," Josh said, pulling his shirt back on. He explained

how they'd gone to see the young falcons, only to find the nest empty.

"Well, this is a young peregrine, all right," the vet said. "Pretty rare around here."

Doc found the band on Flash's leg and cut it off. Then he gently spread the falcon's wings and probed for broken bones.

"He seems healthy enough," Doc said. "Probably just starting to fly. But lookee here. Someone's trimmed his wing feathers!"

The kids crowded around.

"See?" the vet continued. "Peregrines normally have long, pointy wings. These have been rounded off with scissors."

Just then, a tall woman with black hair came up to the table. "What's everyone looking at?" she asked.

"Oh, hi, Grace," Doc said. "Kids,

this is my new assistant, Grace Lockwood. Grace, these kids brought in a young peregrine."

The woman gave the kids a long look. Her eyes were piercing. They reminded Dink of an eagle's eyes.

She turned and ran her hands over the bird's back. Suddenly, Flash bit her finger. "Ouch!" she said.

The vet chuckled. "Better wear your gloves, Grace."

"What should we do with him?" Josh asked.

"I'll keep him here for a couple days," Doc said. "We'll make sure he's okay. Then we can decide what to do."

The kids said good-bye and headed back to Main Street.

"Well, at least he'll be safe there," Josh said. "I wonder where the other two are."

"Wherever Flash was before he escaped!" Ruth Rose said.

"What I want to know," Dink said, "is why someone would trim Flash's wings."

"Why don't we ask Curt?" Josh said. "He knows a lot about falcons."

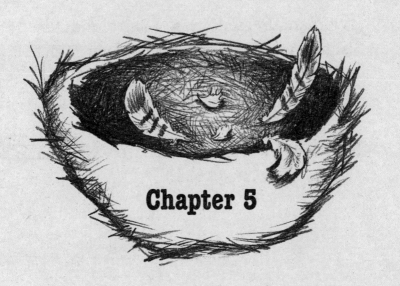

Chapter 5

A small sign on the side of the fire station said DEP—DOWNSTAIRS. A green arrow pointed the way. At the bottom of the stairs, the kids came to a door that said DEPARTMENT OF ENVIRONMENTAL PROTECTION.

No one was in the office. There were a few desks and a bunch of file cabinets against one wall. A stuffed owl in a glass case stood on a counter.

Just then, the door opened and a

woman dressed in a T-shirt and tan shorts walked in. "Can I help you?" she asked the kids.

"We're looking for Curt," Josh said.

"Mr. Striker usually goes home to eat lunch," she said. "Do you want to come back later?"

"It's kind of important," Josh said. "Does he live in Green Lawn? We could walk over."

The woman pointed to a map of the town on the wall. "He's new here, but I think he's renting a cabin out on Bridge Lane. Do you know where that is?"

"Sure," Dink said. "He must live near the river, right?"

The woman nodded. "That's right. Just look for his brown pickup truck."

The kids left the fire station and hiked over to Bridge Lane. There were only a few houses in this part of town. Most of them were surrounded by trees and thick shrubbery.

"That must be it," Josh said. They were standing in front of a wooden fence near a group of pine trees. A gravel driveway cut through the trees, leading to a small cabin.

"Look, there's a brown truck," Dink said.

When the kids walked through the gate, they saw Curt Striker sitting on the cabin's small porch. He was eating a sandwich.

Curt jumped down off the porch

and headed toward them. "Hi, kids,"
he said. "What brings you way out
here?"

Josh told him about how they'd
found one of the baby falcons in the
woods.

"Not only that," Ruth Rose said, "someone put a tag on his leg and clipped his wings!"

"Really?" Curt said. He looked thoughtful. "Sounds like I owe you an apology, Josh. A person *did* take that falcon."

Josh grinned shyly.

"Why would someone clip his wings?" Dink asked.

"Well," Curt said, "the most likely reason is that someone was training him to do something."

"Like what?" asked Ruth Rose.

Curt shrugged. "Could have been a lot of different things."

While they talked, Curt walked them back toward Bridge Lane. "Where is this falcon now?" he asked.

"We took him to the vet," Josh said. "Doc Henry said he'd take care of him."

Curt nodded. "Thanks for letting me know. I'll be sure to check in with Doc Henry."

The kids said good-bye and headed back toward Main Street.

"I hope he catches whoever took those falcons," Ruth Rose said. "Cutting a bird's feathers off is just plain mean!"

Josh nodded. "Yeah, but at least it doesn't hurt. I think it's like cutting your toenails."

They walked past Ellie's Diner. Grace Lockwood was sitting at the window, reading and eating lunch. When she noticed the kids watching her, she stared back at them through the glass.

Her face was blank, but her eyes made the kids hurry away.

"She looks upset about something," Ruth Rose said.

"Maybe she just doesn't like kids gawking at her while she eats," Dink said.

"Did you guys see what she was reading?" Josh asked.

"Some magazine," Dink said.

"Not just some magazine," Josh said, looking at Dink and Ruth Rose. "I recognized the cover. It was *Falconry Today*."

Chapter 6

"I think Josh is sick," Ruth Rose whispered to Dink.

"I am not sick," Josh said. He took another bite of his tuna sandwich.

The kids were eating lunch at Dink's picnic table.

"Then why are you so quiet?" Ruth Rose asked. "You haven't insulted me all day!"

Josh chewed his sandwich. "I'll insult you later," he said. "Right now

I'm thinking about those missing falcons." He looked at his friends. "I think Grace Lockwood took them."

"Grace Lockwood!" Dink said. "Why do you think it was her?"

"You saw that magazine she was reading," Josh said. "It was all about falcons."

Ruth Rose nodded. "She *was* acting a little strange at Doc Henry's."

"Yeah, and remember how she looked at us at Ellie's," Josh said. "She was staring right at me."

"Staring at you?" Dink said. "Josh, she stared at *us* because we were staring at her!"

Josh snitched one of Ruth Rose's carrot sticks. "Let's go back to the vet's and talk to her," he said. "Maybe she'll say something that'll be a clue!"

Dink got up to go. "Okay, but I think you're wrong, Josh. Just because

Grace Lockwood reads magazines about falcons doesn't mean she goes around robbing nests."

At the vet's, the kids peered through the window at Grace Lockwood.

"Look!" Josh whispered. "She's wearing long leather gloves! Falconers wear gloves like that!"

"So do firefighters," Dink said.

They went inside. Grace Lockwood was holding a crow down on a table. The bird had plastic wrapped around its leg and neck.

She looked up. "Yes?" she asked.

"Um, we came to see how Flash is doing," Ruth Rose said. "What happened to the crow?"

Grace shook her head. "Plastic six-pack holders!"

The kids watched as Grace carefully snipped the plastic with scissors.

The crow bit her gloves several times. Dink shuddered. That beak looked sharp!

When the crow was untangled, Grace moved toward the rear of the building. "Will one of you get the door for me?"

Dink opened the door and held it. Grace carried the crow through a small courtyard that was filled with cages and pens.

She threw the black bird into the air. "And stay away from plastic!" she yelled. The crow disappeared into the trees.

Dink looked around the yard. It was as big as a basketball court and surrounded by a tall wooden fence with a gate.

Dink saw a sleeping skunk in one cage. Other cages held raccoons and rabbits. He saw a few snakes and a lot

of birds. He even saw a baby fox!

"I always thought vets just took care of cats and dogs," Josh said.

"Some do," Grace said. "I happen to like wildlife."

Josh looked at Dink and Ruth Rose and wiggled his eyebrows.

"Where's Flash?" Josh asked, looking around at several other cages.

"I put him over here," she said, walking toward a corner of the courtyard. "Doc likes to separate the newcomers from the other animals."

Grace stopped in front of a cage covered by a small rug. "He may be sleeping," she said.

She removed the rug. The bottom of the cage was covered with straw. Inside was a section of hollow log.

"That's where he goes to hide from us," Grace said. She tapped lightly on the side of the cage.

"That's strange," she said, opening the cage door. She jiggled the log, then peered inside.

"What's the matter?" Ruth Rose asked.

"He's gone," Grace said.

Chapter 7

"What!" Josh looked into the cage. "How could Flash be gone?"

"I don't know," Grace said. "I'd better tell Doc."

She hurried toward the office.

"Something's fishy here," Ruth Rose said. "How could Flash just disappear?"

"Someone stole him again!" Josh said.

Doc Henry and Grace ran across

the courtyard. The vet was peeling off a pair of surgical gloves.

"He was in his cage before lunch," Grace said.

Doc Henry bent over and looked into the cage. "Darndest thing," he muttered. "Was the gate locked?"

Grace nodded. "I think so, but I'll check." She ran to a corner of the courtyard. "The lock's been busted!"

Doc and the kids hurried over. The thick wooden gate was closed, but the lock had been shattered. Bits of wood and metal were on the ground.

Doc Henry picked up the pieces of the lock. "Somebody sure wanted to get in here," he said. "That lock was the best on the market!"

Dink examined the door closely. "I wonder if there are any fingerprints on the wood," he said.

"Could be," the vet said.

"Should we call Officer Fallon?" Dink asked.

"That's an excellent suggestion," Doc Henry said. He walked back toward his office.

"I'd better get that lock fixed," Grace said. She hurried away without saying good-bye.

The kids left. They walked past Crystal Pond back toward Main Street.

"I'll bet Grace busted that lock to make it *look* like someone broke in," Josh said.

Dink shook his head. "Grace helps animals, Josh."

"Do birds have memories?" Ruth Rose asked suddenly.

"Why?" Dink asked.

"Well, remember when we first brought Flash to Doc Henry's office? Flash bit Grace on the hand."

"Yeah, so?"

Ruth Rose stopped walking and looked at Dink and Josh. "Well, if Grace climbed the tree and took those falcons, maybe Flash remembers her. Maybe that's why he bit her!"

"You guys are jumping to conclusions," Dink said. He pushed the cross button at Main Street.

"I think we need more information about peregrine falcons," he added.

"Dink's right," Ruth Rose told Josh. "If we know more about them, maybe we'll be able to figure out why someone's taking them."

"Why don't we go to the library?" Dink suggested, crossing Main Street.

"Okay," Josh said, "but Grace Lockwood is still at the top of my list!"

"Who else is on your list?" Ruth Rose asked.

Josh jogged across the street. "Nobody!"

Chapter 8

When the kids entered the library, Mrs. Mackleroy was gluing a cover onto a book.

"Hi, kids," she said. "Someone loves this book so much they wore the binding right off!"

She finished the job, then laid a heavy book on top of the glued one to keep it flat. "There," she said, wiping glue from her fingers. "So how can I help you today?"

"We're looking for information about falcons," Josh told her.

Mrs. Mackleroy pointed to the computer table. "Do you know how to do a computer search?" she asked.

"Sure, we do it in school all the time," Ruth Rose said. "Come on, guys!"

Dink sat at the computer. Josh and Ruth Rose looked over his shoulder. Dink typed in F-A-L-C-O-N-S, then hit the "enter" key.

A few seconds later, a long list of book titles appeared on the screen.

"Geez, there must be fifty books about falcons," Josh said.

"Try PEREGRINE," Ruth Rose said. Dink typed in the new word, and the list shortened. The library had four books about peregrine falcons.

Dink printed the shorter list, and they took it to Mrs. Mackleroy.

"These are in the children's room," she said, making check marks next to two of the titles.

The kids found one of the two books. The title was *Peregrine Falcons: Royal Raptors*. They huddled together on a bench and quickly turned pages.

The book talked about how peregrine falcons had nearly been wiped out because of pesticides.

They flipped more pages until they came to "Amazing Falcon Facts."

"'Peregrine falcons are easy to train,'" Josh read aloud.

"And look, it says they mate for life," Ruth Rose added.

"Look at fact number seven," Dink said, running his finger down the page. "'Peregrine falcons are among nature's fastest hunters. When chasing birds, peregrines have been known to top 200 miles per hour!'"

"That's faster than a cheetah!" Josh said.

"My dad's car only goes a hundred," Dink said. "Boy, wouldn't it be neat to see peregrine falcons racing."

"THAT'S IT!" Ruth Rose yelled.

Mrs. Mackleroy tapped her pencil on her desk. "Ruth Rose..."

"Sorry," Ruth Rose said.

The kids returned the book and hurried outside.

"I bet someone is stealing falcons to

race them!" Ruth Rose said. "People race dogs and horses, so why not falcons?"

"Let's tell Curt," Josh said. "He doesn't even know Flash was stolen again."

They called the DEP office from the phone booth in Ellie's Diner. Josh told Curt that someone had broken into the vet's and stolen Flash. Then he told him about what they had learned in the library.

A few seconds later, Josh hung up. "He's coming right over."

"He is?" Dink said.

"Yeah," Josh said. "And while we're waiting, I could use a pistachio cone!"

Ruth Rose ordered her usual: strawberry. Dink got his favorite, butter crunch. The kids sat in a booth and worked on their cones.

"You know, I've been thinking,"

Ruth Rose said between licks. "Who besides us knew that Flash was at the vet's?"

Dink and Josh looked at her. "Well, Mrs. Wong knew," Dink said.

"For sure, *she* didn't break in and steal Flash!" Josh said.

"And Doc Henry knew, but I don't think it's him, either," Dink said.

Ruth Rose glanced at her friends. "Who else?"

"Grace Lockwood!" Josh said.

"Don't forget about Curt," Dink said. "We told him that Flash was at Doc Henry's."

Josh shook his head. "It's Curt's job to *protect* wildlife."

Just then, Curt Striker walked into the diner. He ordered a cup of coffee, then slid into the booth. "So you kids have been doing some detective work, eh?" he said.

"Someone stole Flash right out of the vet's place!" Ruth Rose told Curt.

"I know," Curt said. "Josh told me on the phone. But who's Flash?"

She grinned. "The falcon! We named him that because he eats so fast."

"So what's this about racing falcons?" Curt said, looking at Josh.

"Well, we read that peregrine falcons can fly 200 miles an hour!" Josh said. "So we thought someone might be training them to race."

Curt sipped his coffee. "Racing falcons, eh? That's an interesting idea."

"Could someone make money racing falcons," Dink asked Curt, "like in a horse race?"

Curt nodded slowly. "Yes, I guess they could."

He finished his coffee. "Tell you what, let me run your idea by a few of

my contacts. Meanwhile, let's just keep this between us, okay?"

"Do you really think you can find out who took the falcons?" Ruth Rose said.

Curt slid out of his seat. "You can count on it," he said.

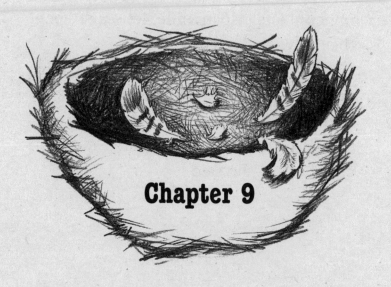

Chapter 9

The kids stepped outside Ellie's and saw Officer Fallon standing on the corner.

"Hi, kids," he said. "What're you doing on such a nice day?"

"Hi, Officer Fallon," Dink said. "Did Doc Henry call you about the break-in?"

Officer Fallon pushed the "walk" button on a traffic light pole. He was carrying a small black case. "I was just

heading over there with my fingerprint kit," he said. "The doc told me about these disappearing falcons. But how are you kids involved?"

Josh filled him in on how he'd been watching the falcons' nest.

"When we went to look yesterday, the falcons were gone," Ruth Rose said.

"And we think we know who did it!" Josh said.

Interrupting each other, Josh and Ruth Rose explained how they thought Grace Lockwood was stealing falcons and training them to race.

"Well, *I* don't think it's her," Dink said.

Officer Fallon nodded slowly. "I tell you what," he said. "When we get there, let's just watch and listen." He smiled. "Maybe we'll all learn something."

Officer Fallon and the kids walked into Doc Henry's outer office. Through the window, they could see him and Grace putting a cast on a dog's leg.

"It would be neat to be a vet," Josh said. "You get to play with animals all day."

"It's not play, Josh, it's hard work," Officer Fallon said. "Some vets get called out in the middle of the night! Besides, I thought you wanted to be a bird artist."

Josh grinned. "Couldn't I do both?"

Doc Henry came out, wiping white plaster dust from his fingers. "Thanks for coming over," he said to Officer Fallon. "Come on, I'll show you what's left of my lock."

The kids watched Grace lift the dog off the table. She carried him to a cage and gave him a dog cookie.

"You guys are wrong about Grace," Dink whispered. "She really likes animals."

"Lots of crooks like animals," Josh reminded Dink.

Ruth Rose nudged them. "Come on. Let's go watch Officer Fallon get finger-prints."

The problem was, there were none. Officer Fallon spread the dust, but no prints appeared. "Well, I guess he wiped the door or wore gloves," Officer Fallon said.

"Or *she* wore gloves," Josh muttered.

Dink remembered something else. "Mrs. Wong said there were tiny letters on the leg band," he said to the vet. "Did you read them?"

"I sure did, Dink. Come on inside and I'll show you."

Officer Fallon and the kids crowded into the office. Grace Lockwood was filling out some papers at the desk. Josh stared at her until Dink gave him a lit-tle shove.

"Hand me that leg band, would you, Grace?" the vet asked.

Grace nodded and gave the band to Doc Henry. The vet picked up a magnifying glass from his desk and handed it and the leg band to Dink. "Tell me what you see, young man."

Dink peered at the band through

the glass. "Letters and numbers," he said.

"Can you read them?"

"'GLKS-6-17,'" Dink read. He looked up. "What does it mean?"

Doc Henry took the band and the glass.

"The letters are a mystery to me, but the numbers may be dates," he said. "If I'm right, the numbers mean Flash was born on 6/17—June 17th."

"Could the letters be the initials of the person who took Flash?" Josh asked.

"That's good thinking," Doc Henry said. "Those letters *could* be initials. But whose?"

"Without any fingerprints," Officer Fallon said, "I'd say our thief has gotten away free as a bird!"

Dink stole a look at Grace. Her name tag stood out against her white jacket. Maybe the GL on the leg band stood for Grace Lockwood!

Dink gulped. Was Josh right? Was Grace Lockwood kidnapping falcons after all?

Chapter 10

The kids walked Officer Fallon back to the police station on West Green Street.

"So are you going to arrest her?" Josh asked.

"Arrest who, Josh?"

"Grace Lockwood!" Josh said.

Officer Fallon smiled and shook his head. "We don't have any proof that she's done anything wrong."

Dink decided not to say anything about the GL initials on the band. Josh

was already trying to throw Grace Lockwood in jail!

"Don't worry, Josh," Officer Fallon continued. "I'm sure we'll catch whoever's doing this."

The kids watched him walk into the station. "Come on," Dink said. "Let's go to the petting zoo for a while."

"Dink, don't you care about the falcons?" Josh asked.

"Sure I care. But you heard Officer Fallon," Dink said, crossing West Green Street. "We don't have any proof that it was Grace Lockwood."

Josh kicked at a stone. "Trust me, you guys. There's something weird about her!"

Dink laughed. "Josh, you just think she's weird 'cause she caught you staring at her cheeseburger!"

The kids cut around the library and entered the zoo. Llamas and baby deer nibbled pellets from kids' hands. A goose waddled along in front of six goslings. There were a few animals in cages, but most were loose.

Several teenagers walked around selling animal food. They wore dark green shorts and shirts with big round badges. The badges said GLPZ, for Green Lawn Petting Zoo.

"Wait a sec, guys," Ruth Rose said. "I want to feed the fawn."

Dink and Josh watched her hurry over to one of the teenagers.

"Well, I still think Grace Lockwood's the one," Josh insisted. "We should tell Curt about her."

"Tell him what, that she gave you a dirty look?" Dink asked.

"For one thing, I'm gonna tell him about the initials on that leg band," Josh said. "He might know what they mean."

Ruth Rose came back with a small

bag of pellets. "Want some?" she asked Dink and Josh.

"Better not give any to Josh," Dink said. "He might eat 'em!"

"Haw haw," Josh said, taking a few of the pellets from Ruth Rose's bag.

They fed the deer and the llamas, then left the zoo.

Josh called Curt Striker's office from the lobby of the Shangri-la Hotel.

He hung up. "Not there."

"Now what?" Ruth Rose said.

"Let's go to his cabin again," Josh said. "If he's not there, we can leave a note."

"Saying what?" Dink asked.

Josh dug a pencil out of his pocket. He got a piece of paper from Mr. Linkletter, the hotel clerk, and wrote on it.

"This," he said, showing the paper to Dink and Ruth Rose.

FOR CURT STRIKER:
FLASH'S LEG BAND HAS
GLKS 6-17 WRITTEN ON IT.
I THINK I KNOW WHAT
THE GL STANDS FOR.

JOSH PINTO

Dink stared at Josh. "What do you think GL stands for?" he asked.

Josh grinned. "Grace Lockwood!"

"But what about the KS?" Ruth Rose asked.

Josh shrugged. "That's what we'll ask Curt. Come on!"

The kids hiked up River Road to Bridge Lane. Halfway there, Ruth Rose suddenly stopped.

"What's the matter?" Dink asked.

She was staring into space. "Something's bugging me. It was something I saw at the DEP office, but I can't remember what!"

"Maybe it was that stuffed owl," Josh said. He made big owl eyes at Ruth Rose.

"No, I think it was something I saw on a desk." She stomped her foot in the dusty road. "Why can't I remember?"

A few minutes later, they reached Curt's cabin. Josh walked up and knocked on the door.

There was no answer.

"Guess he's not home," Dink said.

"Maybe he's in the backyard," Josh suggested. "Let's take a look."

The backyard was empty except for a pile of firewood.

Ruth Rose pointed to a dirt path that led into the woods. "Maybe this is how he got to the tree yesterday," she said.

Suddenly, they heard a low whistle.

"What's that?" Josh said.

"Just someone calling his dog," Dink said. "Come on, let's get out of here. We're trespassing."

The whistle sounded again. Josh started running up the path. "That's a falcon!"

Dink and Ruth Rose followed Josh. They found him standing in front of a small shed. On one side, a window flap had been propped open.

"Listen," Josh whispered.

The kids heard tweeting sounds and more whistles coming from the shed.

"There are falcons in there!" Josh said. He ran around the side and started tugging at a thick padlock on a door.

"Stupid thing is locked!" Josh said.

Ruth Rose went back to the window. "Boost me up, guys."

Dink and Josh crisscrossed their arms. Ruth Rose climbed on and hoisted herself up. "There are about ten cages in there filled with falcons!" she said.

Josh and Dink let her down.

"I'm going inside," Josh said.

"We're going with you!" Ruth Rose said.

A wooden barrel lay in the tall weeds a few yards away. The kids rolled it over and stood it under the window.

Standing on the barrel, Josh was able to crawl through the opening.

Ruth Rose went next. Then Dink.

The inside of the shed was cool and dark. In the dim light from the window opening, Dink counted at least a dozen falcons in cages.

The birds flapped their wings and let out low whistles. Their dark eyes watched the kids' every movement.

Suddenly, the light from the window was blocked. Curt Striker was glaring in at them!

"You brats just couldn't mind your own business!" he said. "You had to snoop, didn't you?"

Then his face disappeared. A moment later, the window flap slammed shut.

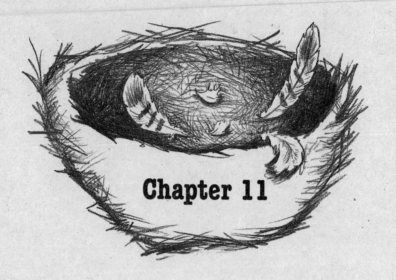

Chapter 11

Dink stared at the spot where daylight had been. He could feel Ruth Rose and Josh come closer.

"What if he doesn't let us out?" Ruth Rose asked.

"Let's try to get that window flap open again," Dink said.

Dink and Josh hoisted Ruth Rose up to the window. She shoved against the flap. "Forget it," she said. "He must have locked it."

They tried pushing against the door, but it too was solidly locked.

"What're we gonna do, guys?" Josh asked. "No one even knows we're here!"

Dink walked around the dim shed, feeling the walls for openings. In one corner, he stumbled over some rakes and shovels.

"Guys, look!" Ruth Rose said suddenly.

"Look at what?" Josh asked.

"On the floor, by my foot," she said.

Dink looked down and saw a round spot of white.

"Sunlight!" Josh said.

They looked up. There was a small hole in the roof.

Dink ran to the corner and grabbed a shovel. "Maybe we can bust through!" he said.

Josh took a rake. Together, they

tried to poke at the small hole.

"I can't reach!" Josh said.

"Some of these cages are empty," Ruth Rose said. "Maybe you could stand on them!"

Together, Josh and Dink dragged four cages over and made a platform. Standing on it, they found that they could easily reach the ceiling.

They smashed at the hole. After a few minutes, it was the size of a softball. Hunks of wood, shingle, and tar paper fell on their heads and shoulders.

Dink stopped to wipe his eyes.

"My arms are killing me," Josh said, sitting on the cages to rest.

"At least now we can see better," Ruth Rose said. She walked around, looking at the caged falcons.

"The cages all have labels," she said. "The first two initials are different, but the second two are always KS."

"Guys, I found Flash," Dink said.

He was looking at a cage holding three young falcons. The label on the cage door read GLKS-6-17.

"OH MY GOSH!" Ruth Rose yelled. "I just remembered what I couldn't remember!"

"What?" Dink asked.

"When we went to Curt's office, I saw a nameplate on his desk," she said. "His name is spelled with a K, not a C!"

"I don't get it," Josh said.

"I do," Dink said. "The KS on Flash's leg band stands for Kurt Striker, right, Ruth Rose?"

"Right! And I bet the GL stands for Green Lawn!" she said.

"Now I get it," Josh said. "He labeled the falcons with the place he found them and his own initials."

"We have to tell Officer Fallon," Ruth Rose said.

"First we have to get out of here!"
Josh grabbed his rake and climbed back
on the stack of cages.

With Dink and Josh both smashing
at the roof, they made the hole larger.
Sunlight poured in on their sweaty,
dirty faces.

Finally, the hole was wide enough
to crawl through.

"Pile up more cages!" Ruth Rose said.

With two more cages on the stack, the kids could climb out onto the shed roof.

They sat for a minute, breathing in the clean air and feeling the sun on their faces.

"It was him the whole time," Josh said, sounding disappointed.

"At least we found the falcons," said Dink.

Josh walked to the edge of the roof and looked down. "The barrel's still there," he said. "Come on, we can climb down."

As soon as they were on the ground, the kids ran toward Main Street and the police station.

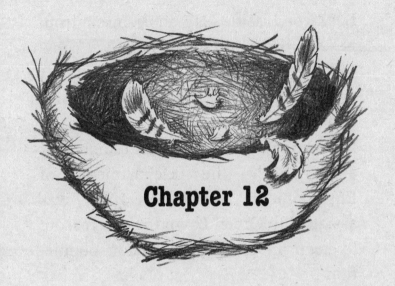

Chapter 12

An hour later, it was all over. Doc Henry, Grace Lockwood, and Officer Fallon sat with the kids in a booth at Ellie's Diner.

"They caught Kurt Striker in Massachusetts," Officer Fallon said. "He's sitting in a jail in Springfield right now, waiting to be shipped back here."

"So he took the falcons from the nest?" Josh asked.

"Not only that nest, Josh," Grace

Lockwood said. "He took birds from nests in three other states that we know of."

Doc Henry smiled. "I think we owe you kids an explanation," he said. "Grace isn't a vet. She's an undercover agent with the Department of Environmental Protection. She was assigned to Green Lawn for one reason: to keep an eye on our falcon population."

Josh stared at Grace. "I knew there was something weird about you!"

Everyone laughed. "Grace knew about the nest," Officer Fallon told Josh. "And she knew that you were out there a lot with your binoculars."

"I watched you watching the falcons," Grace said. "At first I thought *you* had taken them."

"You thought it was Josh?" Dink said. "He thought it was you!"

"I know," Grace said, smiling at Josh. "You kept looking at me funny!"

"Did you suspect Kurt Striker?" Ruth Rose asked.

Grace shook her head. "Not a clue. We have you kids to thank for figuring that out."

"So what was he doing with the falcons?" Dink asked.

"You kids were right about that one, too," Doc Henry said. "Striker had a little business going. He was taking young falcons and training them to race."

"What will happen to them?" Dink asked.

"We'd like to set them all free," Grace said. "But they've had a lot of human contact, so they probably wouldn't make it in the wild. Don't worry, there are plenty of wonderful zoos that keep animals happy and safe."

"Maybe Flash could live in the

Green Lawn Petting Zoo!" Josh said.

"Now, there's a great idea!" Doc Henry said. "I'll talk to them about adopting all three from Flash's nest."

"As for Kurt Striker, he'll spend some time in jail," Officer Fallon said. "He'll no doubt rat on a few of his cronies, and they'll join him."

Ellie came over carrying a large tray. "Ice cream on the house!" she said. "I brought vanilla for every—"

"But I always get pistachio!" Josh said.

"You didn't let me finish, Josh," Ellie said.

"You'll have to excuse Josh," Ruth Rose said. "He gets cranky when he's hungry."

"And he's *always* hungry!" Dink added.

"As I was saying," Ellie went on, "vanilla for everyone except Joshua

Pinto, the boy who saved our falcons!"

She set a huge dish of pistachio ice cream in front of Josh. "And I want you to eat every bite," she said, smiling.

"Don't worry about Josh," Dink said. "That'll be gone in a flash!"

A to Z Mysteries™

Dear Readers,

I've always loved animals. My brother and I used to find orphaned animals in the woods behind our house. We brought home baby squirrels, bunnies, even an owl. My dad helped us build cages for the animals, and my brother and I took care of them until they were old enough to go back to the wild.

For my ninth birthday, my parents gave me a pair of binoculars. From that day forward, I became a bird-watcher, just like Josh! I kept a journal of the birds I saw. I even drew pictures of the birds and labeled them.